You're Doing That in the Talent Show?!

BY
Lynn Plourde ✳ ILLUSTRATED BY Sue Cornelison

DISNEY • HYPERION / LOS ANGELES • NEW YORK

Library of Congress Cataloging-in-Publication Data
Plourde, Lynn.
You're doing *that* in the talent show?! / by Lynn Plourde ;
illustrated by Sue Cornelison.—First edition.
pages cm
Summary: Penelope, an exuberant hippo, and Tiny, her cautious mouse friend, plan their act in the school talent show.
ISBN 978-1-4847-1491-1
[1. Talent shows—Fiction. 2. Hippopotamus—Fiction. 3. Mice—Fiction. 4. Friendship—Fiction.]
I. Cornelison, Sue, illustrator. II. Title. III. Title: You are doing that in the talent show?!
PZ7.P724Yl 2016
[E]—dc23   2014049056
Reinforced binding
Visit www.DisneyBooks.com

With love to Josh,
my truly talented son-in-law
—L.P.

For my grandson Alder,
with love
—S.C.

"*Shhhhhhh!*" hushed Tiny. "You're making a scene."
"Of *course* I'm making a scene," said Penelope. "Soon
we'll *all* be making a scene. Look! The
SCHOOL TALENT SHOW!"

Tiny giggled. "It *was* fun last year. This year *you* are old enough to be in the show too, Penelope."

"Yes! We can do an act TOGETHER!" said Penelope.

"Um . . ." Tiny hesitated.

"Oh, come on," begged Penelope. "A best-friend act would be . . . the BEST!"

"I'll think about it," said Tiny.

"There's no time for thinking, Tiny," said Penelope.
"We don't have a minute to waste. Let's go practice
at my house."

"Do you have any ideas?" asked Tiny.
"Dance! Ballet is my best talent!"
said Penelope.

"You're doing **THAT** in the Talent Show?!
Count me out," said Tiny.

"Then maybe a different kind of dance," said Penelope.

"Oh, yes!" said Penelope.

"Oh, no!" said Tiny.

"Oh, yes, yes!" said Penelope.

"Oh, no, no!" said Tiny.

"Then what do YOU suggest?" asked Penelope.
"Let's sing in the school chorus," said Tiny.
"You did that last year, Tiny. I could barely see you in the back row. Do you think they'd let *me* be in the front row?"

"Er . . . maybe not," said Tiny.

"I know! We could put on a skit," said Penelope. "My favorite story—Rapunzel!"

"You're doing **THAT** in the Talent Show?! Count me out," said Tiny.

"How about a different story?" asked Penelope.
"Jack and the Beanstalk?"

"Oh, yes!" said Penelope.

"Oh, no!" said Tiny.

"Do YOU have another idea?" asked Penelope.

"The chorus is still
the best idea," said Tiny.
   "Do you think they'd let me sing a solo?"
asked Penelope.

"Um . . . maybe not," said Tiny.

"Then let's do a circus act," said Penelope.
"I've always wanted to be a trapeze artist!"

"You're doing **THAT** in the Talent Show?! Count me out," said Tiny.

"Then *what*?" demanded Penelope.
"Chorus! I already told you," said Tiny.
"Singing in the back row of the school
chorus is NOT spectacular," said Penelope.

"Penelope, you don't have to be
spectacular *every* day," said Tiny.
"I don't?" Penelope looked shocked.

After Tiny left, Penelope started in on her training.

Do-re-mi-mi-MEEEEEEE!

Penelope called Tiny. "I've been practicing," she said.
"Practicing what?" asked Tiny.
"Practicing singing and *not* being spectacular," said Penelope.
Tiny giggled. "That must be hard for you."
"It is," agreed Penelope. "But I want to be in the Talent Show with *you*."
"In the chorus? With me? Really?" asked Tiny.

"Yup," said Penelope. "Best friends stick together."

On the day of the show, Penelope shouted, "YIPPEE!"

Tiny shook his head. "There you go again."

"Don't worry," said Penelope. "I'm excited to be in the Talent Show with YOU!"

"I've been thinking," said Tiny. "Why don't you do one of your other acts? We'll still be in the show together, just in different parts. I can clap for you, and you can clap for me."

"Really?" asked Penelope. "You wouldn't mind?"

"No, but which act would you do?" asked Tiny.

"My ballet-Rapunzel-trapeze act, of course!" said Penelope. "I've been practicing, just in case the audience wants an encore."

Tiny shook his head. "Somehow, that does not surprise me."

Before the two friends could wish each other luck, the Talent Show started.

"Oh, yes, yes!" shouted Penelope as she clapped louder than anyone for Tiny and the chorus.

Then it was Penelope's turn.
The audience oohed and aahed.

"Oh, **no, no**!" said Tiny. "She's stuck!"

Tiny did what any
best friend would do . . .

"You were spectacular!" Penelope whispered to Tiny.

"And so were you . . . as always," Tiny whispered back.

"Should we keep bowing?"
asked Penelope.

"Oh, yes, yes!"
said Tiny.

TIPS FOR A SPECTACULAR PERFORMANCE

- **Practice makes perfect.**
  Whatever your performance is—whether it is singing, playing an instrument, giving a speech, or something else—you should practice over and over until you feel comfortable and confident.

- **Get used to an audience.**
  Perform your act in front of a group of friends or family members. Afterward, ask them if they have suggestions about how you could improve your performance.

- **Use an "outside recess" voice.**
  You don't want to shout, but when you sing or speak before an audience, you want to *project* your voice so that everyone can hear you.

- **Face the audience.**
  When you perform, the audience wants to SEE you, so make sure your shoulders are square toward them. Then you can turn your head—not your body—to talk to other performers while still facing the audience.

- **The show must go on.**
  Things happen. Scenery falls. Someone forgets his or her lines. A hippo gets stuck on a trapeze. No matter what happens, keep performing as best you can. The audience doesn't know how it was *supposed* to happen, so they might not even notice the mistake!

- **Be polite, not smug, and don't apologize.**
  When your performance is over, people will likely compliment you. You should say "Thanks! Glad you enjoyed it." But no one wants to hear someone brag, "Wasn't I great?" Saying you're great isn't so great. On the other hand, if you made a mistake, there's no need to apologize. You did your best and that's what everyone wants to remember.